...investigates

The mystic moustache

by Kate Pankhurst

Look out for more books about
Mariella Mystery

The Ghostly Guinea Pig

A Cupcake Conundrum

The Huge Hair Scare

The Curse of the Pampered Poodle

The Spaghetti Yeti

A Kitty Calamity

The Disappearing Dinner Lady

Mariella Mystery

Investigates

The mystic moustache

by Kate Pankhurst

Orion
Children's Books

ORION CHILDREN'S BOOKS

First published in Great Britain in 2016
by Hodder and Stoughton

1 3 5 7 9 10 8 6 4 2

A CIP catalogue record for this book is available from the British Library.

ISBN 978 1 4440 1236 1

Printed and bound in Great Britain by Clays Ltd, St Ives plc

The paper and board used in this book are from well-managed forests
and other responsible sources.

Orion Children's Books
An imprint of Hachette Children's Group
Part of Hodder and Stoughton
Carmelite House
50 Victoria Embankment
London EC4Y 0DZ
An Hachette UK Company

www.hachette.co.uk
www.hachettechildrens.co.uk

For Jenny Glencross,
a true Mystery Girl!

my
moustache
collection

CHOOSE
CLUES

I
LOVE
mystery

♡?

tip toe

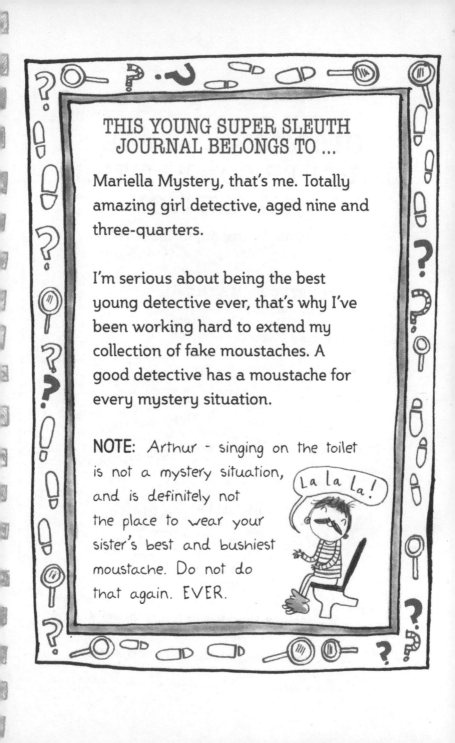

THIS YOUNG SUPER SLEUTH JOURNAL BELONGS TO ...

Mariella Mystery, that's me. Totally amazing girl detective, aged nine and three-quarters.

I'm serious about being the best young detective ever, that's why I've been working hard to extend my collection of fake moustaches. A good detective has a moustache for every mystery situation.

NOTE: Arthur - singing on the toilet is not a mystery situation, and is definitely not the place to wear your sister's best and bushiest moustache. Do not do that again. EVER.

La la la!

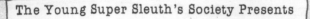

The Young Super Sleuth's Society Presents

THE YOUNG SUPER SLEUTHER COMPETITION & CONVENTION

Calling all Young Super Sleuths!

MYSTIC MOUSTACHE MAYHEM!

Witness the talents of the best Young Super Sleuths as they compete to become this year's Young Super Sleuther Champion.

TOP SECRET!

Uncover classified information about famous detectives and infamous master criminals in the Young Super Sleuth Experience.

THRILLS!

Ride the Bone Rattler, search the Gruesome Crime Scene Investigation Area and survive the Dodgems of Doom! (If you dare.)

LOCATION: Known Mystery Hotspot, the town of Puddleford, Puddleford Park.

DATES: Monday 6th August – Thursday 9th August

Sunday 5th August

NOTE: Poppy has finished our competition outfits, ready for tomorrow! Eeeek! I'm so excited. Having a distinct Mystery Style is an important part of looking like the Young Super Sleuther champions we want to become.

cool hats

yellow trench coats

2:15PM
**PUDDLEFORD PARK, FINAL MYSTERY GIRL
YOUNG SUPER SLEUTHER PRACTICE SESSION
COMPLETE.**

I can totally imagine it. Crowds cheering and cameras flashing as Young Super Sleuther winners – the Mystery Girls – are presented with the gleaming golden Mystic Moustache trophy.

Or I *could* totally imagine it – until our last practice session, which did not go according to plan.

OPERATION WIN MYSTIC MOUSTACHE

THE TEAM:

VIOLET MAPLE: Mystery Girl with an eye for detail – has checked that our Mystery Kit contains everything we need fifty-seven times. (Good job she did, or we would have forgotten to pack fake moustache glue.)

Violet searching the mystery kit

moustache glue

POPPY HOLMES: Mystery Girl on a mission to win! I bet none of the other teams had a preparation schedule like the one Poppy designed. She says we can't be sure what mystery-solving challenges we'll face, so the only way to win is to be good at everything.

Poppy and her magnifying glass.

THE SCHEDULE

MARIELLA MYSTERY (ME):

Mystery Girl with her eyes on the Mystic Moustache trophy. I just need to stay calm when the competition gets tough and remember that I am a brilliant detective.

me, with my cool hat

The mystic moustache

TARGET: THE MYSTIC MOUSTACHE

The trophy is famous (and not just in the detective world) because so many of the young detectives who have won it have gone on to solve high-profile mysteries and become famous. It's worth millions because it's made from a block of gold presented to the Young Super Sleuth Society seventy years ago, for catching the Bejewelled Bandit (stole jewels from film stars).

Bejewelled Bandit

TASK: UNDERCOVER SURVEILLANCE SKILLS

1:00PM: As planned, the Mystery Girls rendezvous* at Puddleford Park on our bikes to practise undercover surveillance on park users.

our bikes

*RENDEZVOUS: A French word, which sophisticated detectives like us use. It's a fancy way of saying meeting up.

1:01PM: We stop to take in the sight of enormous Young Super Sleuther marquees being set up behind a fence in the centre of the park, knowing that tomorrow we won't be practising - we'll be competing for real.

1:02PM: The serious moment is shattered when a familiar squeaky voice shrieks from the park entrance - "MARIELLAAAA! WAIT FOR MEEEEEE! I WANT TO JOIN IN!"

ARTHUR MYSTERY:

Annoying younger brother who is desperate to be a Mystery Girl. (He never will be.) I told Mum and Dad that the Mystery Girls need to prepare for the competition, but they insisted on bringing along Arthur for a nice picnic.

Arthur. Being annoying

I don't have time for sausage rolls - and I definitely don't have time for Arthur!

1:06PM: Poppy says that Arthur might be quite useful. What is she going on about? There is

Annoying

no way we can perfect our undercover surveillance techniques (which involve a lot of sneaking around quietly) with Arthur here.

1:07PM: Poppy tells Arthur his task is to try and escape from us on his scooter so we can practise a high-speed chase situation.

14

1:08PM: We let Arthur have a head start - as far as the swings - before we follow him.

1:11PM: Arthur is screaming, "I'M A MYSTERY GIRL, WHEEEEEEE!" We must catch him.

1:15PM: Wind whooshes in my ears and my legs burn. Arthur is surprisingly fast. I hear Mum shout in the distance that we need to slow down. Never.

1:16PM: Without warning, Arthur's brakes screech and he stops in front of us, next to an ice-cream van. Violet and Poppy scream. I pull my brakes, but it's too late.

1:18PM: We CRASH into the side of the ice-cream van. Bottles of raspberry sauce and hundreds and thousands topple from the serving hatch onto our heads.

Arthur shouts, "MUMMMM! CAN I HAVE AN ICE LOLLY?"

1:19PM: Before I can untangle myself from my bike, on the road outside the park I see an official-looking black minibus approaching. I realise, with horror, that it has the Young Super Sleuth Society logo on the side.

1:20PM: I hope nobody guesses we are competitors (no serious detective walks around with hundreds and thousands in their hair), but our bright yellow detective coats are a huge giveaway.

1:21PM: I see for the first time the faces of the rival young detective agencies we'll be competing against. Most stare at us, puzzled, but two boys snigger from the back window of the bus as it passes.

1:22PM: Final Young Super Sleuther practice session abandoned. Operation Emergency Clean-Up Mystery Outfits Using Mum's Wet Wipes commences.

LEVEL OF COMPETITION READINESS: WINNERS DON'T LET STUFF LIKE THIS HAPPEN! WE ARE PROCEEDING INTO THE FIRST COMPETITION CHALLENGE WITH EXTREME CAUTION.

NOTE: Hopefully this was just an Arthur-related glitch. (Never, ever let Arthur join in with Mystery Girl activity.)

WORKING IN PARTNERSHIP

Certain mystery situations, such as those spanning a large geographical area or requiring specialist skills you do not have, may be best solved by joining forces with another young detective agency. Getting used to the way that others work can

Lets see if you are as good as you say you are

Hey, partner

be tricky – don't let a potentially perfect partnership end up an awful association.

Teamwork: Top Tips

Using a **secret handshake** can be a great way to cement friendships between detective agencies.

I know a MUCH better way to do it.

Others may have **different investigative methods** to you, that doesn't mean that they are wrong. Avoid being discouraging.

Rivalry can ruin relationships. Instead of getting jealous, see what you can learn from each other.

Be **understanding** that other young detectives may have different schedules to the ones you are used to.

Respect privacy. Do not search your partner agency's Mystery HQ while they are in the toilet. Nobody likes a nosy-parker.

WARNING

Not all young detective agencies have good intentions when they seek to work with you. In rare cases they may wish to spy on you in order to steal ideas, or because they work for an enemy! Remain vigilant.

my bedroom

6:15PM
MY BEDROOM, MY HOUSE, 22 SYCAMORE
AVENUE.

Once we'd cleaned most of the raspberry sauce
from our outfits, Poppy calmed down and said
that it's fine that we didn't meet our competition
rivals looking cool and mysterious because now
they might believe we aren't much of a threat.
Little do they know that – most of the time – we
are totally amazing detectives.

We are cool and mysterious

The Young Super Sleuth's Handbook does say that if things have gone well for a while, like our other practice sessions have, it can make you complacent.*

*COMPLACENT: Thinking, well, I've been amazing at creative disguises, undercover surveillance, clue detection and gadget design, so of course we'll win the competition, when actually you can't relax - not even for a second - because the Young Super Sleuther competition will throw something at you that will blow your Mystery Senses into a million squiggly pieces.

my mystery senses

Whenever I find myself worrying about whether our detective skills won't be as good as the other competitors', I have to remind myself that seven hundred and three young detective agencies entered the competition. Only five were selected – and one of them was us!

Three weeks ago, the Young Super Sleuth's Society called to say we'd got a place and that our application form had really stood out!

(I had a spooky moment and totally knew the second the phone rang it would be about the competition. Dad says that's because I'd thought every phone call since posting our application form was going to be the Young Super Sleuth's Society. But I'm still taking it as a good sign that my Mystery Senses are working well.)

intriguing evidence

On the form we'd listed all the complicated mysteries we've solved (there have been loads now), and made sure we included some intriguing evidence, along with pictures of ourselves looking highly professional.

Every year, the Young Super Sleuth's Society chooses the hometown of one of its members to host their competition and convention, so we provided loads of information and newspaper clippings about mysterious locations we'd investigated in Puddleford.

In fact, thinking about it, I can't believe I was surprised when the Young Super Sleuth's Society agreed that Puddleford was the perfect place to host the event!

MYSTERIOUS LOCATIONS IN PUDDLEFORD

Sinister swing

Puddleford Theatre

EMPTY HOUSE

allotments

Deserted Path

SPOOKY SKIP

Hang on – Mum's calling me for dinner. The Young Super Sleuth's Handbook says that an empty stomach can lead to a loss of focus. I can't risk that before tomorrow.

my Dinner

broccoli

Potato

Sausage

Peas

6:45PM
MY BEDROOM, AGAIN.

I only managed to eat half a sausage and a piece of broccoli at dinner because I feel so nervous and excited all at the same time.

I've read about previous Young Super Sleuther competitions in the Young Super Sleuth's Newsletter. The challenges sound totally difficult, but they also sound totally mysterious. Every day I wake up hoping something mysterious will happen to me, so these could be the most amazing four days of my life!

The thing I'm most looking forward to is the Expect the Unexpected Challenge. That's where the judges test the contestants to their absolute limit with a surprise task. You'd think contestants would get a bit better at expecting something unexpected is going to happen – that's what being a detective is all about – but it always seems to catch them off-guard.

Last year, during a challenge to search a haunted house, each detective agency had a member unexpectedly kidnapped. They had to investigate the paranormal activity and find out what had happened to their missing team members.

Realistic haunted house

One detective couldn't handle it and was found wrapped in a shower curtain in the bath, squeaking that he didn't want to be a detective any more.

traumatised

I'd like to think nothing like that would ever happen to a Mystery Girl, but Violet says even the most advanced young detectives can go to pieces when their every move is being watched by a massive audience and super star detective judges.

SUPERSTAR Judges

ELLE LUSIVE: Known as the Mystery Mover, she is famed for combining gymnastics and disguise. When she isn't undercover, she wears a sparkly cat suit, just in case she has to give acrobatic chase to a criminal or cartwheel to the scene of a crime.

Elle Lusive being bendy

Tartania Mc Snuff

TARTANIA MCSNUFF: Scottish detective who specialises in mysterious creatures. She is reported to have come close to catching the Loch Ness Monster. Wow. I hope she's designed some challenges that involve looking for mysterious creatures.

Loch Ness MONSTER

Elle and Tartania are past winners of the Mystic Moustache and they are AMAZING detectives. I hope the Mystery Girls can follow in their footsteps.

We won't be able to bring the actual Mystic Moustache home if we win – because it's so valuable, and being young detectives, we don't have the right level of security in our HQ to make sure nobody steals it. Instead, our names will be etched into the trophy and then we will bring home a very realistic rubber replica that we can put on display.

Until then, I've drawn a life-size picture of it and pinned it next to my bed to focus my mystery-solving mind.

The mystic moustache

Monday
6th August

I'm READY

**9:30AM
YOUNG SUPER SLEUTHER COMPETITION AND
CONVENTION SITE, PUDDLEFORD PARK.**

WE ARE HERE! This is actually happening!

Walking into the competition site was like
entering a dream world of mysteriousness.
Terrified screams filled the air (from the Bone
Rattler Ride in the Zone of Mystery) and a sea of
shimmering, golden moustache-shaped helium
balloons bobbed above the heads of the crowd.

Me, Poppy and Violet had just enough time before the first challenge to hurry through the Young Super Sleuth Experience Marquee and catch a glimpse of the Mystic Moustache trophy.

We knew we must be close because a massive crowd had gathered in a small, very dark room and there was lots of oohing and ahhing. The crowd might not have been detectives, but I could understand why they were so excited. It's not every day that a piece of mystery-solving history like this comes to Puddleford. (Or that we get the chance to win it!)

I pushed my way to the front, pulling Poppy and Violet with me, and managed to peek around the security guard who was telling people to stay behind the rope.

The trophy stood in a huge glass display case, a bit like a very fancy goldfish in a tank. Spotlights shone on it, and beams of light twinkled from the points of the twirly moustache. If you looked really closely, you could see the tiny names of winners carved into its base.

That's when it felt real. That's when I realised just how huge it would be for the Mystery Girls' names to be on that trophy. (That's also when I felt a bit sick because my tummy started doing nervous cartwheels, a bit like the sort Elle Lusive can do.)

10:45AM
YOUNG SUPER SLEUTHER BACKSTAGE AREA,
MEETING OUR COMPETITION RIVALS.

I think I'm doing an OK job of making it look as
if I'm cool and collected, even though we are
in a room filled with the country's best young
detective agencies.

When Elle Lusive and Tartania McSnuff
introduced themselves, my tummy did the
biggest acrobatic backflip so far.

sparkly →

Tartan
(mystery
kit

"Helloo, competitors," said Tartania in her soft Scottish accent. "Seeing you all waiting to start your Young Super Sleuther journey brings back happy memories."

"Ah, yes, winning the Mystic Moustache was one of the best moments of my life too," said Elle, grinning. "Now I hope you're feeling ready for the challenges ahead? There's nothing to be nervous about. Is there, Tartania?"

Poppy nudged me. Violet looked terrified. They both knew that what Elle actually meant was: *You should be nervous, very nervous.*

Worried

After that, Elle and Tartania left to prepare for the first challenge and told everyone to get to know one another. It was an excellent opportunity to suss out the competition. Here's who we are up against:

THE COMPETITORS

THE BAFFLEMENT BOYS:
Linus and Pip. I suspected
they were going to be
trouble when they laughed
at us yesterday. Linus said,
"Oh, when we saw you
in the park, we assumed
you must be amateurs, not

Bafflement Boys

competitors." WHAT? Just because they can do
a really good Mystery Eyebrow* does not mean
they are better detectives than us.

BEST MYSTERY EVER SOLVED: Prevented
the theft of a priceless spoon from their
local art gallery. A spoon? Doesn't sound
that impressive.

spoon

*MYSTERY EYEBROW: Using your eyebrows to
look ultra-suspicious. I can do this, but only for
short periods of time. Pip's and Linus's eyebrows
seem to be fixed in that position.

mystery
eyebrow

THE SUSPICIOUS SISTAS: Manesha, Kiki and Dot. Not actually sisters and they don't seem that suspicious, they seemed more interested in high-fiving us and shouting, "GO, SISTA!" really loudly.

matching glittery hoodies

The Suspicious Sistas

BEST MYSTERY EVER SOLVED: Revealed that a haunted shoe shop was not haunted at all. It was just the shop owners trying to attract attention by levitating stilettos on invisible thread. (Doesn't sound too difficult.)

haunted stilletos

DARLENE DANGERFIELD:
Didn't smile once, and annoyingly, she's managed to get the rare Young Super Sleuth badge that says, 'DANGER IS MY MIDDLE NAME'. (Well, it's not, it's her last name.)

Darlene looking moody

DANGER IS MY MIDDLE NAME

BEST MYSTERY EVER SOLVED: Refused to tell us! Said it was top-secret information. Hmmm. More like she hasn't ever solved any decent mysteries.

Jess, Ben and Bobby

GIVE US A CLUE: Jess, Ben and Bobby. They aren't much older than Arthur, so can't be a real threat. Even so, Violet says we shouldn't underestimate them.

BEST MYSTERY EVER SOLVED: Exposed a child in their class who was stealing crayons in all the best colours - silver, gold and fluorescent pink. Simple stuff.

Crayons

refreshments

2:05PM
YOUNG SUPER SLEUTHER BACKSTAGE AREA,
BREAKTIME. FIRST CHALLENGE COMPLETE.

Tartania and Elle have called a short break
because they can't decide who should win the
first challenge. I don't think it will be us.

"Contestants," Elle said, when we were all lined
up on stage. "Your first Super Sleuther Challenge
is ..."

My heart raced. The whole of Puddleford was
expecting to see stunning detective work.

"... To build a Mystery HQ suitable for a detective agency serious about becoming a Super Sleuther Champion. You have three hours. GO!" Tartania continued.

Lights flashed and a heavy black curtain behind us lifted, revealing five rooms, one for each team. There were sparkling silver containers lined up in front of the rooms, overflowing with furniture, fabric and detective equipment.

Even though I know loads of stuff about what a HQ should have in it, because we spent ages perfecting the real Mystery Girl HQ, I had the sudden feeling that I had completely forgotten it all. Linus from the Bafflement Boys didn't hesitate. He dashed past us, grabbed a lamp from one of the containers and sprinted into their HQ.

Everything happened in a blur. The audience whooped; Poppy grabbed equipment while I arranged it; Violet shouted out things we have in Mystery Girl HQ: "INTRUDER ALARM! QUIET ZONE! EVIDENCE INSPECTION TABLE!"

When the announcement came that the challenge was complete I had to tell myself to breathe – our HQ looked totally amazing, just like the real Mystery Girl HQ does. We had a cool old-fashioned mystery desk and a huge pin board. But ...

"WHERE did the Suspicious Sistas get that hammock?" Poppy said, staring at their beach-themed relaxation zone. "I'm sure we've done enough ... OH NO!"

Beach-themed relaxation zone

Poppy pointed at the Bafflement Boys' HQ next.

They'd managed to build an enormous bookshelf neatly stacked with items from their super-cool gadget collection. I couldn't believe I'd thought our beanbag chill-out zone would be enough!

Looking at the amazing touches in the other rooms, I got a horrible sinking feeling that our ideas just weren't as good.

Any minute now we'll have to go back out there. What if we come last?

Darlene's concealed hiding place

Give us a Clue's door →

GIVE US
a
CLUE
DETECTIVE AGENCY

2:20PM
YOUNG SUPER SLEUTHER COMPETITION
STAGE. IN CHAOS!

I was ready to expect the unexpected, but I don't think anybody was prepared for what has just happened! (And I'm not talking about who won the first challenge.)

Returning to the stage to hear the results, I hoped we looked as professional as Tartania did. Elle Lusive wasn't with her, but I thought maybe she was going to come on stage doing a celebratory backflip when the winner was announced or something.

"And the winners are … The Suspicious Sistas!" Tartania said. "Well done, Sistas – the beach is the perfect place to think about whodunnit!!"

The Suspicious Sistas started dancing and high-fiving each other.

A leader board flashed up on the big screens at the side of the stage. The Bafflement Boys took second place (they did not look happy) and the Mystery Girls (phew) took third. Darlene Dangerfield came fourth and looked furious. Give Us a Clue didn't take the news that they had come last well. Bobby fell to the floor sobbing.

Anyway, none of that seems to matter. Not after what happened next.

Elle Lusive suddenly appeared on the big screens. She was cartwheeling towards us down the dark corridor in the Young Super Sleuth Experience.

"There's still everything to play for, competitors!" she said, flipping upright. "Now, I've got something to show you that will focus your Mystery Senses ..." She tiptoed through the Young Super Sleuth Experience, as if she was on an undercover mission.

"I don't like this!" whispered Violet. "It's the Expect the Unexpected Challenge – I don't think I can handle anything else today."

But it wasn't that.

"This is what being a Young Super Sleuther is all about – THIS is what you are working for!" Elle said, beckoning the camera to follow her into the tiny dark room we'd visited this morning. "Behold, the world-famous Mystic Mou—"

Elle froze. An expression of dark suspicion flashed over her face. (Exactly like the one I've tried to copy from pictures of her in the Young Super Sleuth's Newsletter.)

The camera jerked from Elle to the Mystic Moustache's fancy stand. Spotlights still shone above it, but now the only thing they lit up was a jagged hole in the glass display case.

I made an emergency detective deduction.

NEW MYSTERY ALERT: THE MYSTIC MOUSTACHE HAS BEEN STOLEN!

Dark Suspicion

KNOW YOUR CRIME: THEFT

Ensure you are familiar with the tell-tale signs indicating that a theft has occurred. Acting quickly means you can be following clues before a victim even realises a treasured item has been stolen. (Everyone loves a detective who solves a crime before it's reported.)

Top Ten Signs a Theft Has Occurred:

1. Hysterical victim screaming they can't find their handbag/shoes/sofa.

2. Gap on wall of an art gallery.

3. Person sprinting while pushing an overflowing shopping trolley.

4. Speeding ice cream van (could be a getaway car).

5. Suspicious burglar alarm maintenance worker.

6. A surprisingly light diamond tiara (could be a fake).

7. A car full of sheep. (Sheep rustling)

8. A bike that no longer works as it should.

?

9. A distressed dog, may have been dog-napped.

awoooh!

10. Discovering a bath full of money.

small fortune

TOP TIP

Don't overreact. Somebody borrowing a small invaluable item, like a pencil sharpener, does not mean you need to launch a full criminal investigation.

YOUNG SUPER SLEUTH COMPETITION STAGE,
MYSTERY HQ (THE ONE WE JUST BUILT).
EMERGENCY MYSTERY GIRL TEAM MEETING.

It wasn't just me who deduced what had
happened to the Mystic Moustache. Gasps
rippled round the arena. The Suspicious Sistas'
smiles had been replaced with looks of deep
shock. Darlene Dangerfield was shouting at Give
Us a Clue to stop screaming.

Bobby
Hysterical

Annoyingly, the Bafflement
Boys managed to keep the
same I'm-a-serious-and-
suspicious-detective expression
they'd had all morning. They
weren't doing anything useful,
though. Poppy and Violet shot me a
glance that said, Emergency Mystery Girl Team
Meeting needed – NOW.

A crew member ran across the stage and
whispered to Tartania. I knew things must be
bad, because although Tartania has come face
to face with the Loch Ness Monster, it took her a
moment to compose herself enough to speak.

"I have been asked to inform you all that
the entire Young Super Sleuth site is closing
immediately," she said. "The disappearance of
the Mystic Moustache is being investigated by
Elle, and I am about to join her. We hope that the
competition will continue as planned tomorrow,
but a further announcement will be issued in due
course."

The curtains closed, muffling the frantic gossiping of the audience. Crew members were ushering us backstage so parents could come and collect us. The Bafflement Boys dashed off first. I hoped this was a sign they weren't perfect all the time and were actually desperate for a hug from their mums to get over the trauma of the missing Moustache. (The Mystery Girls are made of stronger stuff.)

Nobody noticed me, Poppy and Violet duck into the HQ we'd just built. (The perfect place for an emergency Mystery Girl team meeting.)

"This is a disaster," Poppy said. "We only got third place – if the competition is cancelled, all our hard work will be for nothing!"

I knew we were better than third place too, but I couldn't believe Poppy thought that was more important than the theft of a world-famous priceless golden moustache! (Potentially the biggest mystery situation the Mystery Girls have ever faced.)

"We need to figure out who took the Mystic Moustache and get it back, or there might not even *be* a Young Super Sleuther Competition," I said.

"Yes, this could ruin the Young Super Sleuth Society's reputation!" Violet said. "They are meant to be the world's best young detective society and the Mystic Moustache has been stolen from under their noses! Embarrassing alert!"

I hadn't even thought of that, but Violet was right. The Young Super Sleuth's Society has taught us everything we know about mystery-solving. We can't stand by and let everyone think they are amateurs. (Or that the Mystery Girls have been trained by amateurs!)

"Let's start with some logical explanations," I said.

The Young Super Sleuth's Handbook says that logical explanations should always come before dashing off to do anything else – they help you formulate a plan. Without a plan you are just people running around picking up random things from the floor.

Logical Explanations:

(Shocking But Possible) Explanation
One: A competitor stole the Mystic Moustache because they know, deep down, that they are not good enough to win it. Could one of them have sneaked off during the toilet break and hidden the trophy to collect when the coast is clear? Under a dodgem? In their Mystery Kits?

Contestants who visited the toilet at break

Pip

Jess

Darlene

manesha

But none of the other contestants' Mystery Kits looked noticeably heavy just now. And would any of them really want to risk their detective careers by stealing it? Would they attempt such a thing with totally amazing detectives Elle and Tartania watching?

? →

heavy

(Probable) Explanation

Two: A master criminal stole the Mystic Moustache so they could sell it – or because they have a grudge against the Young Super Sleuth's Society.

The trophy is famous, so lots of people might want to steal it. Also The Young Super Sleuth's Society must have annoyed plenty of criminals over the years who want revenge. Our list could be quite long.

(Practically Impossible) Explanation

Three: Elle Lusive said that the day she won the Mystic Moustache was the best of her life. Maybe she's secretly always wanted it back? And stole it while the film crew wasn't looking?

Elle Lusive doesn't need the Mystic Moustache! She has won loads of trophies for her detective work and is at the top of her career!

VERDICT: Elle Lusive wasn't on her own for long enough to steal the Moustache and she has no motive, unlike other suspects. We can rule her out but we need more evidence to narrow our suspect list further. We need to search the scene for clues that could reveal the identity of the thief, or point to the current whereabouts of the Moustache.

Tyre tracks from a getaway car

Sighting of somebody struggling to carry a heavy object

Twinkle of gold from the Moustache's hiding place

NOTE: If the site is closed after today, the trail of clues could go cold - disaster! (We have to get started before Mum, Dad and Arthur arrive backstage to take us home!)

**3:30PM
OUTSIDE THE YOUNG SUPER SLEUTH
EXPERIENCE MARQUEE.**

We might have come third in the Design a
Detective HQ Challenge, but I am awarding the
Mystery Girls first place for our excellent work on
Operation Explore the Experience.

Young
super sleuth
marquee

THE
YOUNG SUPER SLEUTH EXPERIENCE

3.00PM: Outside the backstage exit of the competition arena, I spot Elle and Tartania in serious discussions with Detective Sparks from Puddleford Police. In high-profile cases, detective agencies often work in partnership with the police.

3:05PM: Me, Poppy and Violet use the crowds shuffling towards the exit as cover, and dash past an upturned balloon-seller's cart. Was this pushed over by the criminal as they escaped? Or a failed attempt to hide the Moustache?

3:06PM: I hold my breath as we dart under the crime scene investigation tape and into the dark entrance of the Young Super Sleuth Experience.

EVIDENCE UNCOVERED FROM MYSTIC MOUSTACHE DISPLAY ROOM:

MYSTIC MOUSTACHE DISPLAY CASE: Glass is really thick so must have been smashed with a heavy object, like an iron or a brick or something. (No sign of anything like this.)

tea!

DISABLED ALARM SYSTEM: The alarm control wasn't working and had liquid all over it - a closer inspection revealed this to be milky tea. Does the thief drink tea?

GLITTERY YELLOW FLUFF: Could this have fallen from the Moustache-stealer's belly button?

fluff

wrapper

TOFFEE TWISTER

GOLDEN TOFFEE TWISTER SWEET WRAPPER: Is the thief a toffee eater, or was it dropped by a visitor?

3:15PM: Footsteps approach. A flustered security guard - the same one who was guarding the trophy earlier - pokes his head around the door and asks what on earth we are doing.

3:16PM: Poppy pretends to look really upset (good undercover work, Poppy) and says that we can't believe the Mystic Moustache is gone and we had to come and see it for ourselves.

3:18PM: The security guard (badge says his name is Jim) looks at his feet. Then he says that it's all his fault and he can't believe he fell for a Classic Diversion Technique.* A Classic Diversion Technique? WHAT?!

*CLASSIC DIVERSION TECHNIQUE: When a criminal does something, like tipping over a balloon-seller's cart, causing Jim to leave his post and investigate. Then, while the coast is clear, the criminal steals the Mystic Moustache!

VERDICT: Jim told us that the balloon cart was tipped over at approximately 2:00pm - which means the Mystic Moustache went missing during the toilet break after the Design a Detective HQ Challenge! So the Moustache

time of the crime ↓

definitely could have been stolen by a competitor! Further analysis of the evidence is needed back at Mystery Girl HQ (the one at my house, not the one we've just built).

NOTE: We haven't found any sign of the Mystic Moustache hidden on the convention site. I asked staff on the park gates if they'd seen anyone suspicious. They said somebody could have danced past waving the Mystic Moustache and they wouldn't have noticed because they've been dealing with a crisis.

(A mobility scooter is stuck in a puddle, blocking the exit to the car park everyone is now trying to leave.)

mud

Flopped

Beanbag

5:30PM
MYSTERY GIRL HQ. FLOPPED ON A BEANBAG.

Ugh. We ended up in a traffic jam for ages because of the stupid stuck mobility scooter.

stuck

Mum kept telling us that even if the competition was cancelled, the Mystery Girls would always be winners in her eyes. Hmm. I'd definitely prefer to win the Mystic Moustache. I'm not sure it sounds very official if it's just my mum who thinks we are amazing detectives.

Back in HQ we had lots to discuss.

"It's disappointing that we can't narrow our suspect list yet," I said, "but now we know what time the Moustache was stolen, it confirms we need to keep investigating potential master criminals and other contestants."

Some contestants had the perfect Window of Opportunity* to commit the crime, after all.

*WINDOW OF OPPORTUNITY: A person can only do something terrible, like stealing the Mystic Moustache, if they aren't already busy doing something else. Sneaking off when everyone thinks you are in the toilet, for example, is a perfect window of opportunity.

toilets

"You're right – we need to hope that the competition isn't cancelled. If the site shuts, important clues might be lost and investigating will get tricky," Violet said.

"Definitely," Poppy said. "Some of our prime suspects would be sent home – possibly with the Mystic Moustache!"

No matter what happens tomorrow, we can't leave this case unsolved. That's why we've looked at our current suspects in more detail – The Young Super Sleuth's Handbook says this is an excellent way to be sure you don't miss anything that could be important.

Turn over for suspect line-up

PIP, BAFFLEMENT BOY:
Were he and Linus able to remain calm when they heard the Mystic Moustache had been stolen because they'd always planned for Pip to sneak off and steal it?

A CRAZED MASTER CRIMINAL:
Identity still unknown. Gate staff didn't see anyone escaping, but maybe somebody in Puddleford town centre did? A shop owner or passer-by?

MANESHA CHAUHAN, SUSPICIOUS SISTA:

Is winning the first challenge the perfect cover story? Maybe she stole it to use as a matching fashion accessory for the Sistas' glittery hoodies?

DARLENE DANGERFIELD:

Did she tell Give Us a Clue to get a grip when the Moustache disappeared because them getting upset made her feel really guilty about stealing it?

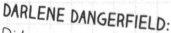

JESS DAVIES, GIVE US A CLUE: I'm not sure she is big enough to smash the display cabinet, or strong enough to carry away the heavy trophy, but appearances can be deceiving.

VERDICT: We can't accuse anyone of this terrible crime without more evidence. Our enquiry will continue to target two types of suspect:

be**lly** button
tea

COMPETITOR TURNED BAD: We need to verify each contestant's toilet visit alibi*, ask about tea-drinking/toffee-eating habits and belly button hygiene.

OTHER CRIMINALS: Eyewitnesses must be sought who may be able to provide a description of any suspicious characters seen in Puddleford.

eye witnesses sought

*ALIBI: A suspect can't be in two places at the same time. If it can be confirmed that they visited the toilet and came straight back, they can be removed from our suspect list.

Tuesday
7th August

Who
took the
mystic
moustache?

Breakfast

milk

COCO PUFFOS

**8:00AM
BREAKFAST TABLE, MY HOUSE, 22
SYCAMORE AVENUE.**

Dad has just passed me this morning's
Puddleford Gazette and the Young Super Sleuth's
Society has issued a statement.

MISSING MOUSTACHE OF MYSTERY!

Yesterday, the Young Super Sleuther Convention and Competition, being held in Puddleford Park, became a real-life crime scene, after the world-famous Mystic Moustache trophy was, we can now confirm, stolen.

Many were stuck in the car park for over two hours while staff struggled to move a mobility scooter that had been abandoned.

Visitors were evacuated from the convention amid scenes of chaos.

Elle Lusive, top investigator and competition judge, has issued this statement on behalf of the Young Super Sleuth's Society:

"I'm pleased to say the convention site will open again today. However, to ensure that myself and Tartania are able to investigate, a number of changes will be introduced:

1. The Expect the Unexpected Challenge is cancelled.

2. The Meet the Judges stand will be closed. (Signed photos of Elle and Tartania still available in the convention shop.)

3. Expensive detective gadgets on display have been removed for safe-keeping.

In the unlikely event the Mystic Moustache is not found, we would like to offer reassurance that the replica rubber trophies to be taken home by winners remain safely in the possession of the Young Super Sleuth's Society."

Should the so-called 'best young detective agency in the world' have been able to stop a theft from right under their noses? Call our news desk with your opinions!

This is so frustrating! I
don't think that Elle and
Tartania should have
cancelled the Expect the
Unexpected Challenge.
What if people say that
winning the competition
was rubbish because there
was no Mystic Moustache and
that it was easier this year, so winners aren't
really amazing detectives?

FRUSTRATED

Even more frustrating, everything that happened
yesterday makes it seem like the Young Super
Sleuth's Society totally don't know what they are
doing – which we know isn't true. That traffic jam
wasn't their fault – it was whoever stupidly left
that mobility scooter in a patch of mud!

Without the Young Super Sleuth's Society and advice from their brilliant Handbook, the Mystery Girls would still be trying to solve the Case of the Fuzzy Fish Finger*.

*THE CASE OF THE FUZZY FISH FINGER: One of our first, very simple, mysteries. An unexplained mouldy fish finger was found on the floor of Mystery HQ. We suspected Arthur had put it there as a joke, but after following Young Super Sleuth advice we uncovered evidence that Watson (pet cat and trusty sidekick) had been pulling things out of the kitchen bin and hiding them for later in HQ.

mouldy fish fingers

It's more important than ever that the Mystery Girls help to restore the good name of the Young Super Sleuth's Society.

9:30AM
YOUNG SUPER SLEUTHER BACKSTAGE AREA.

I should probably be worrying about the second
challenge, but we've been too busy.

When we arrived on-site, we kept our Mystery
Senses tuned in for further clues. The crowds are
smaller today and people look a bit nervous, not
excited like yesterday. The balloon sellers aren't
selling golden moustache balloons any more –
they've been replaced with black question mark-
shaped balloons. Quite fitting, since everybody
is asking questions about where the Mystic
Moustache is and who took it.

Backstage, we waited for the right moment to check toilet alibis.

The Suspicious Sistas were practising their Mystery Victory Dance for when they become Young Super Sleuther Champions. (Yeah, right.) I asked Manesha whether anything weird happened when she visited the toilet during break yesterday. I watched carefully for signs that she felt guilty, but she just folded her arms and flashed Darlene an evil look.

EVil look

"Weird? Only if you count spending the whole time arguing with Darlene Dangerfield," she said. "Darlene said her secret room was loads better than our beach relaxation area. As if! Jess from Give Us a Clue kept telling us to stop fighting and be friends. Grow up!"

If Manesha was with Darlene and Jess in the toilets for the whole of break, none of them had a window of opportunity to steal the Moustache.

I have also observed that Darlene, Jess and Manesha prefer fizzy jelly sweets to toffees and none of them seem to drink tea, therefore we don't need to ask about belly button hygiene. We are striking them off our suspect list.

jelly sweets

That leaves the Bafflement Boys. They aren't eating toffees or drinking tea, but they are acting strangely. Even for them. They seem really twitchy and they keep looking at their notepad and whispering.

"They are probably just preparing for the challenge, like they were yesterday," Violet said.

I don't know – maybe. HANG ON! NO WAY! CLUE ALERT!!

POPPY! VIOLET!

THIS IS NOT A DIARY ENTRY.
THIS IS A WARNING. DO NOT
LOOK AT THE BAFFLEMENT BOYS OR
YOU WILL GIVE AWAY THAT
I HAVE JUST LOCATED
INCRIMINATING EVIDENCE!!!

Bafflement
mystery
↓ kit

WHEN PIP PUT HIS
NOTEPAD INSIDE THAT
MASSIVE RUCKSACK,
I SAW A FLASH OF
SOMETHING GOLDEN.

EMERGENCY DEDUCTION: THE
BAFFLEMENT BOYS ARE
GUILTY. THE MYSTIC MOUSTACHE IS
IN THEIR MYSTERY KIT
AND THEY MUST BE
CONFRONTED.

Mariella xxx

We
must get
it back!

WHAT? Are you absolutely certain?! Let's tell an adult.

Violet x

adults

VIOLET! What are you talking about? I'll grab Linus. Violet - you grab Pip. Mariella - you grab their Mystery Kit!
Good luck, girls.
Poppy x

9:55AM
YOUNG SUPER SLEUTHER BACKSTAGE AREA.

CRINGE ALERT! We might not be the brilliant
detectives I thought we were.

"Why are you staring at us?" Linus said, as we
waited to make our move. Pip folded his arms
and glared at us too.

I gave Poppy and Violet a look that said, 'Let's do
this' and we raced towards them.

guilty?

Violet tripped over Give Us A Clue's Mystery Kit, but still managed to grab Pip's ankles as she fell. Linus tried to push Poppy away so she sat on his knee.

"You can drop the act, Bafflement Boys! We know you stole the Mystic Moustache and we know it's hidden in your Mystery Kit!" I said in my best I'm-a-serious-detective-who-has-loads-of-experience-in-this-type-of-crime voice.

Kiki shrieked in a really over-the-top way and hid behind Manesha and Dot. Elle Lusive and Tartania darted into the room. (Their mystery reactions are so quick.) Everyone else stared at us.

I grabbed the Bafflement Boys' Mystery Kit and almost toppled over. It weighed so much I could barely lift it. My heart raced. The Mystic Moustache was the only thing that could be making it so heavy.

Linus's arms waved uselessly from underneath Poppy. Pip tried to wrestle the bag from my grip so Violet did the only thing she could from her position on the floor – yanked off his shoe and tickled his foot. Pip yelped, released his grip and the top of the rucksack jerked open. There was the glint of gold and then ...

THUD.

I stared at the object lying at my feet. It wasn't the Mystic Moustache. It was a set of golden false teeth.

false teeth

"Step away, Mystery Girl!" Linus snapped at me as he pushed a shocked Poppy off his knee. "Just because you didn't think to search the crime scene immediately after the theft of the Moustache, does not mean you can attempt to ruin our reputation or damage important evidence!"

no mystic moustache!

WHAT?

Pip smirked and dropped the gold teeth back into their Mystery Kit.

"Yeah, while you were sitting around having your little meeting, we were hot on the trail of the thief. We've already informed the judges who our suspect is," he said, raising his already perfectly-positioned Mystery Eyebrow even higher.

"You may as well close your investigation, because it won't take us much longer to find the thief and return the Mystic Moustache, so WE can win it!" Linus said.

I realised then that they hadn't raced off stage after the first challenge to see their mums – but because they'd been heading to search the crime scene. NO!

I wanted to say something clever, but all I could think of was, "*Little meeting?!* We were following Young Super Sleuth procedure! Logical explanations always come before a search!"

Pip rolled his eyes, as if to say that we were such amateurs.

"The Bafflement Boys have learned all there is to know about being a detective, so we make up our own rules," Linus said. "Now, if you could leave us in peace – we were in the middle of a top-secret mystery meeting."

He and Pip folded their arms and flared their nostrils smugly. They were totally enjoying how stupid the Mystery Girls looked in front of the other contestants – and, worst of all, in front of super-star detectives, Elle and Tartania.

massive nostrils

Right now, I'd like to disappear into the shadows, like Elle Lusive can – but I'm not a good enough detective to be able to do that. Just like I'm not a good enough detective to solve this case or to win this competition.

3:00PM
GIRLS' TOILETS, YOUNG SUPER SLEUTHER
BACKSTAGE AREA.

I'm not a rubbish detective. The Clue Detection
Challenge we've just completed has proved that.

For the second challenge each agency had to
search a cool old-fashioned train carriage crime
scene. It was the sort of setting I've read about
in detective stories and it sent my Mystery
Senses into overdrive! I could tell Poppy and
Violet were just as excited as me
by the way they put aside
feeling embarrassed and
threw themselves into
searching for clues.

amazing

We totally would have won if the Bafflement Boys hadn't found their stolen necklace only seconds before we did. If we can almost beat them in this challenge, we can beat them in the next one. And I've decided, they aren't solving this mystery before we do.

While the rest of the contestants are having photos taken for a feature in the *Puddleford Gazette*, me, Poppy and Violet have come to the toilets to discuss our next move.

"It's actually a good thing that we confronted the Bafflement Boys – we can eliminate them from our suspect list and we know about the false teeth. That means we can try to figure out who left them there and why," Poppy said.

"Yeah, at least my Mystery Senses were tuned enough to spot that they had something golden in their Mystery Kit," I said.

"You're right. The Young Super Sleuth's Handbook says that detectives who think they know everything always mess up, so we can't leave it to those Bafflement Boys to get the Moustache back," Violet said. "I can't believe they are making up their own detective rules!"

Totally. If we are going to do this, we carry on the Young Super Sleuth's Handbook way – that's what has helped us solve all our other mysteries. In situations like this, the Young Super Sleuth's Handbook suggests looking again at the evidence. Then you have to decide your next step.

WHAT WE KNOW:

SUSPECTS: After ruling out the other contestants, we now know the thief must be a criminal who wants the Moustache because it's valuable or because they want to damage the Young Super Sleuth's Society's reputation, or both. But who?

NEW EVIDENCE:

A set of golden false teeth.

Weird
false
teeth

EXPLANATIONS FOR TEETH AT CRIME SCENE:

1. Could have been used to smash Mystic Moustache's display case - but why would the thief carry something as strange as golden false teeth?

2. Maybe the thief has stolen other golden objects and accidentally dropped the false teeth as they fled the scene, or couldn't carry them and the heavy Moustache at the same time?

3. Perhaps the thief wears false teeth? It's usually old people who have false teeth, but we've never seen a granny or grandad wearing a heavy set of solid gold teeth before. And would an elderly person be able to lift the trophy and escape?

CRAZY

OTHER USEFUL INFORMATION: The Bafflement Boys said they think that the thief is close by, which means they must have found some evidence to suggest this. What, though?

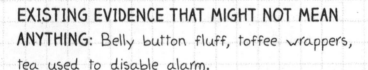

for Bafflement Boy eyes only

EXISTING EVIDENCE THAT MIGHT NOT MEAN ANYTHING: Belly button fluff, toffee wrappers, tea used to disable alarm.

VERDICT: The golden false teeth have given us even more questions - and we need answers! Following up on our plan to seek out witnesses who saw anybody unusual struggling to carry a heavy object yesterday afternoon may help us to reveal the criminal's identity. We are also going to look at some of Poppy's books on famous criminals and crimes to see if any of their descriptions fit our suspect profile.

Missing Mystery Girl alert!

Violet just said something and it made Poppy go crazy.

"I know you'll think I'm mad," Violet said. "Somebody like my granny would struggle to lift the Moustache – but the other evidence sort of fits with the idea that the thief is elderly, doesn't it? My granny wears false teeth and they fall out sometimes if she eats chewy toffees, and she has fluff at the bottom of her handbag, like the fluff we found. And she drinks lots of tea..."

"IT CAN'T BE!" Poppy shouted suddenly. Then she ran off!

CRazy

4:30PM
YOUNG SUPER SLEUTH EXPERIENCE. HALL OF FAMOUSLY INFAMOUS CRIMINALS.

We have just made a TOTALLY AMAZING BREAKTHROUGH!

Me and Violet finally found Poppy in the Famously Infamous Hall of the Young Super Sleuth Experience Marquee.

"Where have you been?" she said. Like we were the ones who'd run off with no explanation.

"Erm, looking for you!" Violet replied. "You ran off and didn't say where you were going."

"Didn't I?" Poppy said. "Never mind that. When Violet said how all the clues we'd found so far

pointed to an elderly suspect, I remembered
something I knew could be important, so I came
here to check it out."

Poppy pulled us past the life-size cut-outs of the
Diamond Diva and the Postbox Pincher, towards
one of an old lady sitting on a sleek black
mobility scooter printed with a swoosh of golden
stars. Her face was framed with shimmering
golden hair. She was wearing a fluffy
I'm-a-nice-old-lady cardigan, but
her piercing eyes gave me the
creeps.

"Meet the Golden
Granny," said
Poppy.

NAME: THE GOLDEN GRANNY (AKA ETHEL BOYSENBERRY)

AGE: 92

GOLDEN GRANNY FACTS:

Has been on the Young
Super Sleuth's Society's Most
Wanted list for over twenty
years, since she retired from
her job working in a jewellery shop and turned
her love of golden trinkets into a life of crime.

the golden granny

* Has stolen valuables including a solid gold
telephone, dog food bowl and even a bathtub.

* The Granny has outsmarted many detectives
featured in the Young Super Sleuth Experience,
including Elle Lusive and Tartania
McSnuff, who joined forces to locate her
after she stole a set of golden bagpipes.

GOLDEN GRIN: Wears a pair of solid gold false teeth, a treasured possession stolen from a dentist to Royalty. Uses her shocking smile to startle victims, before making off with their valuables. (She has strengthened her jaw muscles to be able to hold the teeth in place by chewing toffees.)

argh!

A GOLDEN GETAWAY: Old age and the weight of her jewellery means that the Granny is not able to make speedy getaways. She uses a high-speed mobility scooter to make her escape. Witnesses have reported her recklessly drinking tea from her flask while driving it. She has been known to drive her mobility scooter at speed towards anyone who attempts to apprehend her.

VERDICT: All the evidence suggests that it was the Golden Granny who stole the Mystic Moustache! She is now on the Mystery Girls Most Wanted List!

No wonder Tartania and Elle looked so worried when the Mystic Moustache went missing – they probably realised straightaway that this was the work of the Granny and they should have been far more careful with the trophy. It won't be easy, but perhaps help from some fresh new detectives, like us (not the Bafflement Boys), will mean she is finally caught.

(That mobility scooter we saw yesterday was her getaway vehicle! I missed the golden stars because it was splattered with mud!)

She must be stopped

7:00PM
MYSTERY HQ, MY HOUSE, 22 SYCAMORE
AVENUE.

We needed to make up for lost time, so it
was tempting to start the hunt for the Granny
immediately, but I knew that wandering around
Puddleford hoping to bump into her wasn't going
to work. The only way to track the Granny down
was to have a plan more cunning than she'd
proved herself to be.

"Now we know what the Bafflement Boys meant
when they said they knew the thief was still in
Puddleford," Poppy said. "The Granny
can only walk slowly without
her scooter and is carrying the
Moustache, so she can't have
gone far at all."

struggling

"Don't forget, though, she is a master criminal. She could easily have stolen another getaway vehicle by now," Violet said. "We need to check that Elle and Tartania have secured her scooter – if she's still in Puddleford, it might only be because she's waiting for an opportunity to get it back."

Violet was right. The Golden Granny might have already made her escape, before we even realised it was her we should be looking for.

"We don't know for sure she's still here. But we still need to think – where would a Golden Granny choose to lie low?" I said, hoping we weren't too late to stop her getting away with the Mystic Moustache.

This is where we will target our search tomorrow. (While remaining vigilant for reports or signs of a Granny escape attempt):

VILLAGE HALL: They hold coffee mornings for old people, so there would be a supply of tea and biscuits in the kitchens for the Granny to survive on.

BAA-RMY WOOL SHOP: Grannies like to knit, so the Golden Granny might be hiding in the stock room and sleeping on piles of wool?

BUS STOPS: Maybe the Granny won't risk trying to get her mobility scooter back and will instead attempt to leave Puddleford by bus? (If she hasn't already.)

All I can think about is how the Granny could be on a bus out of Puddleford right now, laughing her head off that she's outsmarted Elle and Tartania again. I bet she is thinking the Mystic Moustache will look really nice in her bathroom, right next to that golden bath she pinched.

97

We can't let that happen. That's why, as well as our search, we'll put up these posters tomorrow morning.

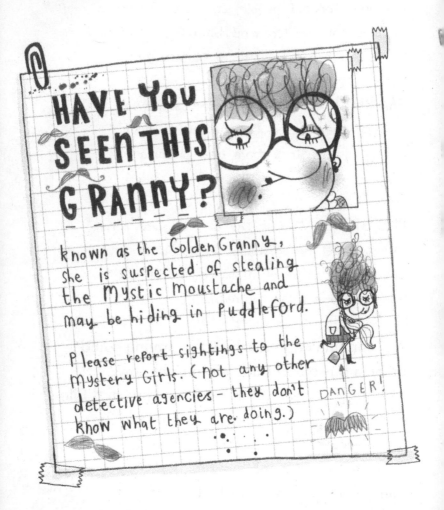

HAVE YOU SEEN THIS GRANNY?

known as the Golden Granny, she is suspected of stealing the Mystic Moustache and may be hiding in Puddleford.

Please report sightings to the Mystery Girls. (Not any other detective agencies - they don't know what they are doing.)

DANGER!

98

Wednesday 8th August

NOTE: As we arrived at the convention I asked the gate staff what happened to the mobility scooter abandoned yesterday. Puddleford police confiscated it - good! That's one less escape method for the Granny, but being a criminal genius, I'm sure she'll figure out another way. I just hope we aren't too late.

9:40AM
YOUNG SUPER SLEUTHER BACKSTAGE AREA,
YOUNG SUPER SLEUTHER CONVENTION.

Bafflement Breakthrough Alert! (Argh! And yay!)

Even though we still hadn't sighted the Granny,
or found anyone who had (bus stops were clear
and there weren't any obvious signs that
BAA-rmy or Puddleford Village Hall had been
used as a hide-out), we'd managed to get
loads done. We put up all our posters around
Puddleford and I was feeling positive we'd hear
from an eyewitness soon.

eye witness

Then, as we walked into the backstage area, I saw Pip elbow Linus, who rushed to fold away the big piece of paper he was inspecting. I read the words 'GOLDEN GRANNY SIGHTINGS', so it must have been a map of Puddleford.

There were gold stars clustered around the centre. One of them had THIS MORNING scrawled in big letters next to it!

THE MAP

"Did you see that? The Granny is still in Puddleford! I can't believe we haven't had any reports yet and they must have ten sightings!" Poppy said.

I wished we had a map full of gold stars too, but at least if the Granny was still here we had a chance of catching her before the Bafflement Boys.

-gold stars

The Bafflement map also revealed some other very important information.

"We thought the Granny would be hard to spot, but she's popping up all over the place," I said. "I think this shows how desperate she is to find another getaway vehicle, something to replace her scooter!"

Poppy and Violet agree that this makes sense. Now I think about it, catching the bus just isn't the Granny's style. It's far too slow, and if anyone spotted she was travelling with the Moustache she'd be cornered.

cornered

BUS →

But what if she finds a new getaway vehicle in the next three hours? We can't stop her while we are busy competing in the third challenge! (Neither can the Bafflement Boys, which is good. But the Granny can't be allowed to leave Puddleford!)

**10:15AM
YOUNG SUPER SLEUTHER BACKSTAGE AREA,
YOUNG SUPER SLEUTHER COMPETITION.**

Good news – the next challenge is going to
be totally useful for tracking the Granny's
movements!

"Two challenges down, two to go!" Elle
announced, when all contestants were gathered
on stage. "Now, Tartania, I've heard there have
been reports of some very strange activity
happening at Puddleford Library."

The Golden Granny, I thought.
It's got to be! But Elle didn't
mean that.

THE GRANNY

"Aye, Elle, I think some Young Super Sleuther Surveillance might be required!" Tartania said. "For the next challenge, you'll be keeping Puddleford Library under close observation – spot the most incidents of suspicious activity and figure out what's really happening and you'll be the winner."

"Tartania and I will be in surveillance positions ourselves, filming your every move and reporting back to the audience," Elle said. "Good luck, competitors, you're going to need it!"

Brilliant! I thought. If the challenge was going to be outside, we could watch for signs of the Granny at the same time. The Bafflement Boys raised their eyebrows at one another, clearly thinking the same thing. Poppy shot me a look that said, we'll show them.

1:15PM
OUTSIDE PUDDLEFORD LIBRARY.

I want to block the details of what just happened during the Surveillance Challenge from my mind, but the Young Super Sleuth's Handbook says a good detective keeps a record of everything. I'm not sure I'm a good detective any more, but I'll write it down anyway.

YOUNG SUPER SLEUTHER CHALLENGE AND GOLDEN GRANNY SURVEILLANCE

10.20AM: We find a hiding place in a large hedge outside the surveillance target - Puddleford Library. It also provides a good view of

other key areas of central Puddleford, so it's excellent for Granny-spotting.

10.45AM: There is no unusual Super Sleuther or Granny-related activity, but we can totally see the other detective agencies' hiding places! Violet is sure that easy-to-detect surveillance positions are an instant point deduction. Darlene Dangerfield is sitting on a bench pretending to read a book; the Suspicious Sistas' bright-pink hoodies are visible in the upstairs window of Roll it Up carpet shop; Give Us a Clue think nobody can see them huddled behind a street sign; and the Bafflement Boys are crouching next to a tiny bin.

PUDDLEFORD TOWN CENTRE

10.55AM: Mrs Finn from Fluff 'n' Feathers pet shop has just walked into the library. She is groaning and limping. Is that meant to be a clue or has she tripped over her pet poodle, Spangle, again?

Limping

11.00AM: Violet starts searching the hedge we are in to check the Golden Granny isn't hiding with us. It causes us to miss part of a distress signal being sent in torch beam flashes from the window of the children's library. All we manage to decode is, 'INVASION, HELP!' What?

11.45AM: Two more people limp into the library. Poppy thinks it might have been set up as an emergency hospital for people involved in a mystery incident. Hmmm. We need more clues.

11.57AM: ARGH! High-pitched screams fill the air. My Mystery Senses leap into action. Give Us a Clue sprint from their hiding place.

11.58AM: I am wondering if we need to move position to get a look at whatever Give Us a Clue have just seen. Then - VROOM VROOM VROOOOM!

11.59AM: A huge sit-on lawnmower, with 'Property of Puddleford Cricket Club' painted on the side, skids round the corner of the library. I don't need my Young Super Sleuth Binoculars to know who is hunched in the driver's seat, her curly golden perm bouncing wildly. The Granny has her new getaway vehicle!

12.00PM: Before me, Poppy and Violet have a chance to move, Linus from the Bafflement Boys throws his notepad at the Granny as she passes their hiding place. It lands, pages fluttering, on her face.

12.01PM: The lawnmower bounces off the kerb, swerves past the bush we are in, and out of view, down Puddleford High Street. The Mystery Girls give chase. I see Linus following behind, but we've got a huge head start.

12.04PM: CRASH! Turning the corner, we see the lawnmower upturned on a pile of squashed vegetables outside Cabbage and Co, the greengrocer's. Then we spot a glimpse of the Granny disappearing down the side of Soapy Suds Laundrette.

ARTIST'S IMPRESSION:
Shimmering hair. Hobbling, as if weighed down by her tangle of golden beads. Sparkling fluffy cardigan. Dragging wheelie shopping trolley – is the Mystic Moustache inside?

12.10PM: Me, Poppy and Violet stand at the top of the alleyway. There is a high wall at the other end and no sign of the Granny. Where did she go?

12.20PM: After three searches of the bins we realise it's no use and that we have lost the Granny.

12.25PM: Back on the street, Elle Lusive is talking to Linus. I attempt to inform her of our Golden Granny sighting and near-miss in catching her, but Linus cuts me off and says that he's already told Elle that after we ran down the alley, the Granny reappeared further up the street, before escaping. Linus saw the direction she was headed and after studying his extensive list of sightings so far, he expects to track her down in the next few hours. *NO!*

12.26PM: Feeling silly, the Mystery Girls turn to head back to our surveillance position, but Elle informs us that she'd actually come to find us because the challenge ended ten minutes ago and we came ... last! DISASTER.

NOTE: All the contestants correctly identified that Puddleford Library was being invaded by ZOMBIES! (Well, Puddleford residents who had volunteered to pretend to be zombies.) That was why people were limping and groaning! Darlene Dangerfield won, and even though Linus chased the Golden Granny, Pip remained in position to watch the library!

SUPER SLEUTHER CHALLENGE OUTCOME: TOTAL FAIL

GOLDEN GRANNY SURVEILLANCE OUTCOME: SIGHTING CONFIRMED, BUT THOSE BAFFLEMENT BOYS ARE TOTALLY GOING TO CATCH THE GRANNY BEFORE WE DO! (ARGH!)

HQ

**4:00PM
MYSTERY GIRLS HQ, MYSTERY GIRL CRISIS
TALKS.**

The Young Super Sleuth's Handbook says that
when mystery-solving is not going according to
plan or (as in this case) is a total disaster, you
should hold an emergency crisis talk to assess
what has gone wrong. That's what we've just
done.

"Something weird is going on," I said. "One
minute the Granny was hobbling around the
corner, the next, she'd vanished! How did
she do that?"

"Mariella," Violet said, "the Golden Granny is a master criminal who has evaded the capture of talented detectives like Elle Lusive and Tartania McSnuff for years. I don't think we should beat ourselves up about not being able to catch her."

"I agree," Poppy said. "We should let the Bafflement Boys find the Granny. They probably have already anyway, and we can focus on winning at least one of the challenges. It's not as good as becoming Super Sleuther Champions, but it would be better than going home as total losers."

Argh! I hate to say it, but I think Poppy is right. We'll never be overall winners now. Winning one challenge would put us in a tie situation with the Suspicious Sistas, the Bafflement Boys and Darlene Dangerfield.

Total loser

So, it's decided. We are officially giving up on the search for the Mystic Moustache. Instead, we are going to concentrate on proving we aren't totally useless detectives by winning a challenge.

Maybe that will be enough to stop the Bafflement Boys' eyebrows going into smarty-pants overdrive when they win, solve the case and become world-famous. Maybe, but I really doubt it.

smarty Pants Overdrive

determined

8:45PM
MY BEDROOM, 22 SYCAMORE AVENUE.

What was I thinking? The Mystery Girls should be the ones to return the Mystic Moustache to its rightful place – and not just because I want to prove something to the Bafflement Boys. The Mystery Girls never give up on mysteries because they are a bit difficult!

The Bafflement Boys keep saying they are about to catch the Granny, but are they really? I can't believe I'm writing this, but it's actually something Arthur did that changed my mind.

I'd thrown my artist's impression of the Mystic Moustache in the bin, so I no longer had to be reminded of how I'd never win it or return it safely from the clutches of an evil granny. I was in a state that the Young Super Sleuth's Handbook calls Mystery Meltdown.*

*MYSTERY MELTDOWN: Extreme confusion where all you can do is lie on your bed and think about the silly mistakes you have made and seriously consider giving up being a detective.

There was only one thing that could cheer me up a little bit, and that was a chocolate bar from the Mystery Girl secret snack supply in HQ. (Clearly marked 'Mystery Girl Treats: HANDS OFF, ARTHUR!') But when I picked up the tin, it felt very light – too light.

I may have been a rubbish detective this week, but I was still able to quickly deduce who was responsible for eating the tin's contents – ARTHUR!

empty!

I ran inside and flung open the door to Arthur's bedroom. He wasn't there. Then I heard the squeaky singing he does when he's using the toilet and I was about to confront him in the bathroom when I spotted something on his bed.

Neatly laid out were three T-shirts. Each one was covered with a jumble of wobbly multi-coloured little hearts and question marks drawn around photos of me, Poppy and Violet.

T-shirts

I looked closer and realised they were photos from previous Mystery Girl investigations that brought back memories of mystery and adventure – and of how amazing it is to solve mysteries with Violet and Poppy. And how good at it we are!

Arthur must have made them for him, Mum and Dad when they come to support us in the audience tomorrow.

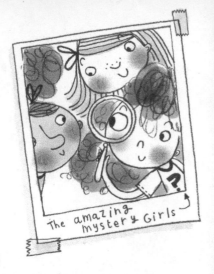
The amazing mystery Girls

I had the weird sensation that I wanted to hug Arthur. (Luckily it passed.) I knew then that I couldn't let the photo we took after the competition finished tomorrow be one of us all looking totally miserable because we had given up on the investigation. What sort of detectives would that make us?

I will, on this occasion, forgive Arthur for entering Mystery HQ, even though there was no need to eat our snacks while he looked for photographs. (I won't be this soppy and forgiving again.)

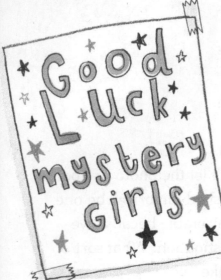

Hmmm. Poppy made me and Violet good luck cards last night. Now I'm not sure I want to annoy her by saying I haven't given up on finding the Mystic Moustache after all.

* I know *
you'll be
B R i l l i ant
as long as
you stay calm
and FOCUS
and
* WIN!
love POPPY
XXX

Thursday
9th August

Have the Bafflement Boys already found the Granny?

11:00AM
GIRLS' TOILETS, YOUNG SUPER SLEUTHER
BACKSTAGE AREA.

I am a terrible Mystery Girl and a terrible friend.
I've let Poppy down by getting distracted by the
Granny – again!

On stage, Elle announced that the final challenge
was a Detective Disguise Challenge. Poppy
let out a sigh of relief. She is the Mystery Girl
Costume Co-ordinator and always makes
amazing disguises. Well, usually.

Detective Disguise Challenge

I spotted Linus glance into the shadows at the side of the stage, before narrowing his eyes and whispering something to Pip. What were they looking at? Had they already found the Moustache?

"MARIELLA!" Poppy shouted.

I turned to see that the curtain had lifted to reveal five dressing rooms. Whizzing through the air, suspended from hooks, were costume-making resources – sparkling fabric, disco balls, cool old umbrellas and giant chunks of foam. Darlene Dangerfield narrowly beat Poppy to grabbing a roll of white sparkly fabric. Oh no. If Poppy hadn't shouted at me she would have got it.

umbrella   fabric   disco ball   box

The Bafflement Boys whisked away tins of paint and some giant fancy picture frames to their dressing room. Kiki from the Suspicious Sistas skipped off carrying a giant piece of cardboard. (The sort of thing you could make loads of cool detective gadgets from.)

cool cardboard

fancy frame

paint

One by one all the best bits of disguise-making equipment were claimed by the other competitors. By the time I leaped into action, the most interesting thing left was a big ball of purple wool. I thought it would be OK when I saw that Violet had a mysterious-looking box. But it was full of ... twigs!

Poppy looked at the twigs, wool and the boring brown fabric we'd ended up with, shaking her head, though she still managed to think of what sounded like an ingenious idea – tree costumes.

twigs

BORING fabric

wool

She started wildly sticking and cutting things, not in her usual genius Costume Co-ordinator way, but in a panicking under pressure type of way. The more Poppy tried to fix things, the worse they got.

Trees would normally be an excellent undercover disguise, but there was no way we were going to be able to sneak up on suspects undetected in these. Our trunks looked more like sausages and our branches flopped about uselessly.

Things got really bad when the Suspicious Sistas peeked out of their dressing room and giggled. We saw that they were going to be three totally cool squashy polka-dot armchairs. Darlene Dangerfield (who was transforming herself into a very convincing human statue) tutted at us and the Bafflement Boys, dressed as half-finished masterpiece paintings – smirked.

Give us a
clue
robots

Even though I was feeling
really jealous of the other
costumes, I was sure that we
could sort out ours.
Unfortunately the pressure got
too much for Poppy and she
ran off stage. Poppy never gets
upset, so we knew this was bad.

POPPY →
upset

The Mystery Girls do not
let members have Mystery
Meltdowns alone. After I had
one yesterday, I should have
spotted she was close to breaking
point. If we can't do this together, we can't do it
at all. That's why we went after her.

Poppy is currently locked in a toilet cubicle
refusing to speak, but I'm not leaving until I know
she is OK. (Or until she agrees to come back on
stage because without Poppy's genius ideas, me
and Violet aren't very good at making disguises.)

11:15AM
OUTSIDE JUDGES' DRESSING ROOM, YOUNG
SUPER SLEUTHER BACKSTAGE AREA.

WEIRD ALERT.

It took ages, but eventually, when I promised to
focus, and Violet suggested that we should make
simple bushes instead of trees, Poppy agreed to
come out of the toilet. That wasn't the weird bit,
though.

Leaving the toilets, something I'd accidentally
kicked bounced off the door of Elle and Tartania's
dressing room opposite. Looking down, I saw
something catch the light.

A small golden bead.

golden
bead

Then, when I looked up I
saw that the door handle of
Elle and Tartania's dressing
room was sparkling.

A closer inspection revealed that it was covered
in a thin layer of golden dust. I'd never seen Elle
or Tartania wear gold make-up before, so what
was this? Something else twinkled below – thin
strands of curled gold scattered on the floor.
They looked very like strands of Golden Granny
hair.

"Mariella, come on – these bushes aren't going to
make themselves!" Violet said from behind me.

I thought about ignoring the weird bits of hair
and gold dust and following Poppy and Violet,
but a totally crazy thought entered my head.
Could the Golden Granny be hiding in Elle and
Tartania's dressing room?

I signalled to Poppy and Violet for silence and pointed to the hair and the dust.

The idea that the Granny might be here reminded me of something I'd read in the Young Super Sleuth's Handbook.

"What if the Granny is using the oldest criminal trick in the book?" I whispered. "What if she is hiding right under the noses of those trying to catch her because that's the last place she thinks anyone will look? Or maybe she's just come back for her false teeth before she leaves?"

We are going in.

THE CUNNING CRIMINAL

Can't find your suspect? Think you've looked everywhere? Think again! Have you revisited the scene of the crime, the place you are sure your suspect must have fled from? If not, a suspect could be using one of the oldest criminal tricks in the book – hiding where you'd least expect them to!

Signs A Criminal May Be Closer Than You Think:

Depleted toilet roll supplies: Toilet rolls may disappear much quicker than usual.

Giggling: Suspect may not be able to contain their excitement that they think they have fooled you.

Te he!

Creaky Floorboards: Could be a sign t suspect is wrigg to get comfy.

Crumbs: The criminal will need to eat.

Extra Squishy Sofa Cushions: Is the criminal concealed underneath?

Ways to Lure a Suspect Out of Hiding:

Sitting patiently

Sit quietly for a long time, thus fooling the suspect into showing themselves because they think you have left the crime scene.

YUM

Place a selection of cream buns in an obvious place. Even a hardened criminal will struggle to find the willpower to resist the delicious smell.

Fling open cupboards and doors with no warning, leaving a suspect no opportunity to dart into their hiding place.

Evacuate!

Shout in a loud, clear voice:
"OH NO! The building demolition team are here."

ARNING

Do not suddenly throw open toilet doors unless you are certain there isn't an innocent member of the public inside. This can lead to embarrassing situations and permanent damage to your mystery solving reputation.

OPERATION GRAB THE GRANNY AND MISSING MOUSTACHE

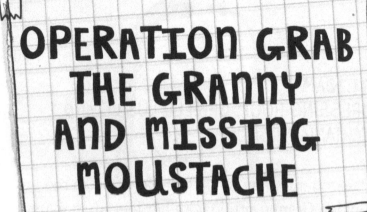

NOTE: Our enquiry took an unexpected turn at this point and I didn't get a chance to write everything down. This is an accurate account of events as they happened.

WARNING: Do not read if you are the sort of person to faint from shock.

clothes rail

11:20AM
DRESSING ROOM OF ELLE LUSIVE AND
TARTANIA MCSNUFF.

Peeking into the room, I half-expected to see the
Golden Granny sitting with her feet up, applying
golden lipstick in Elle and Tartania's mirror. But
nobody was there.

"I don't like this!" Violet said from the doorway.
"We shouldn't be snooping! If we go back now
we can still make some half-decent bushes."

Could the Granny be lurking behind the clothes
rail that was neatly hung with Elle's sparkling
cat suits and Tartania's tartan skirts?
Behind the chaise longue in the
corner? Nothing stirred
in the shadows.

chaise
longue

"Maybe this is a bit silly?" Poppy said.

I thought Poppy and Violet were right, but I decided to have one final check to make sure that the Granny wasn't under the dressing table. Tartania and Elle's Mystery Kits were in the way. I tried to move Tartania's first and ... ooomph!

It weighed a ton, just like the Bafflement Boys' Mystery Kit had when I found those false teeth.

Hmmm.

Opening the Mystery Kit of a world-famous professional detective without asking first would usually be a bad thing to do, but I just needed to know I wasn't going completely crazy.

"MARIELLA!" Violet shouted, "You can't do th—"

She didn't finish what she was saying because inside Tartania McSnuff's Mystery Kit was – the Mystic Moustache.

11:25AM
DRESSING ROOM OF ELLE LUSIVE AND
TARTANIA MCSNUFF, STUNNED.

We all stared. What was the Mystic Moustache
doing in the Mystery Kit of Tartania McSnuff?

"They got it back!" Violet said.
"Tartania must be saving it as a
surprise to give to whoever wins!"

"OH NO!" Poppy said, her eyes wide.
"We should have left the investigating up to
Elle and Tartania all along, then we could have
concentrated on winning it!"

Poppy and Violet must be right – and even though we wouldn't be the ones to win it, I thought at least the Young Super Sleuth's Society would be saved and, even better, Elle and Tartania had found the Granny and the Moustache without the help of the Bafflement Boys!

I leaned forward to zip the bag back up again, before something sticking out of Elle's Mystery Kit, on the floor next to Tartania's, caught the light.

It was a mass of tangled golden hair attached to some netting. A golden wig that looked exactly like Golden Granny hair. The Golden Granny didn't wear a wig, did she?

Wig →

The grins on Violet's and Poppy's faces turned to puzzled expressions as I pulled the zip on Elle's bag fully open and saw that it was stuffed with the Golden Granny's fluffy cardigan, a shimmering skirt and a pair of golden glasses!

"Professional detectives like Elle and Tartania would always put evidence like this into evidence bags," I said. "They wouldn't just shove it in their Mystery Kits."

"Maybe they haven't had a chance to sort it out yet?" Violet said. "Come on, we need to go!"

But how could we, when this was a totally unexpected and strange discovery? I pulled out a tangle of golden beads, like the ones we'd seen the Golden Granny wearing yesterday, except the beads weighed hardly anything. I realised that this wasn't just weird. It was suspicious.

"This stuff can't have belonged to the Golden Granny! The necklace is made of plastic!" I said.

Plastic!

"We were wrong about a few things to do with the Granny," Poppy said. "Maybe she doesn't always wear solid gold?"

Hmmm. The Granny has done a few surprising things so far – taking crazy risks popping up all over town, covering large distances without her mobility scooter – difficult when you are an old lady carrying a heavy golden trophy – so this could be true. I'd also thought that her being able to disappear from that alley when only moments before she'd been hobbling was weird. But now she was wearing fake gold? It was almost as if she was a different Granny.

A different Granny.

A granny who could somersault over a wall. A granny who could show herself, then blink-and-you'll-miss-her-cartwheel disappear. A granny who is not what she seems. Staring at the contents of the two Mystery Kits on the floor, I knew that we hadn't just discovered some nice little surprise.

"We've been looking for the wrong suspect all this time!" I said.

"Erm, what?" Violet said.

I could hardly believe what I was about to say myself, but that didn't make it any less true.

"What if the Granny has done some unusual stuff because she isn't the Granny?" I said. "What if the reason we saw Elle Lusive, only moments after the Granny disappeared yesterday, was because the Granny *is* master of disguise – Elle Lusive?"

Elle Lusive

Poppy clasped her hands to her mouth.

"Elle and Tartania stole the Mystic Moustache and made it look like it was the Golden Granny!" I said.

"Don't be silly!" Violet said. "Elle and Tartania are top detectives. They wouldn't risk their careers, and the good name of the Young Super Sleuth's Society like this!"

Click, click. Click Click.

We heard the unmistakable sound of Tartania McSnuff's heeled boots in the corridor outside.

"Hide!" I said.

There was just time to pull the zips on the open Mystery Kits shut before me, Poppy and Violet hid behind the chaise longue.

WHEN GOOD DETECTIVES TURN BAD

Shocking as it seems, detectives can be driven by greed or revenge or arrogance and turn to a life of crime. Detectives have a detailed understanding of the criminal mind, making them some of the hardest criminals to catch. They know all the tricks to conceal their guilt.

Identifying the Rogue Detective:

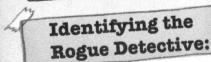

Sneaks off to make 'top secret' phone calls. Could be about an investigation or about a crime they are plotting.

A large backlog of unsolved crimes. Unsolved because they are the criminal behind them?

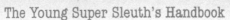

Frequently uses
phrases to cover up
their guilty secret:

I don't know how criminals sleep at night!

If you think I am a criminal you must be a RUBBISH detective.

Whoever committed this crime is a criminal genius.

Goes on solo surveillance missions at the same time as crime sprees are reported.

Not seeming shocked when a terrible crime is reported. Is this because they have seen far worse crimes in the past, or were they behind it all along?

WARNING

While these are all signs of a criminal detective, they can also be signs of a non-criminal detective who is being secretive for good reason, or merely remaining cool in a crisis. You should have solid evidence before accusing fellow detectives of being up to no good.

11:30AM
STILL IN THE DRESSING ROOM OF ELLE LUSIVE AND TARTANIA MCSNUFF, HIDING.

Squeezed between Poppy and Violet, I heard the swish of Tartania's heavy skirt and the door close behind her.

She flopped onto the chaise longue like she didn't have a care in the world. I held my breath and willed Violet not to squeak and give away our position.

FUzzzzZZZ! Fuzzzzz!

There was a crackling sound – a walkie talkie – then Tartania spoke. "Are you in position, Lusive? I repeat, are you in position?"

FUzzzzZZZ! Fuzzzzz

"Affirmative. I'm ready," Elle's voice crackled. "Plan is working. Everyone believes that we've been called to investigate a suspicious incident on-site. Even better, the Bafflement Boys have taken the bait and are about to expose the truth!"

"Aye!" Tartania giggled. "Or what they think is the truth! If the Golden Granny could see us now!"

"Don't!" Elle sniggered. "I might send a photo of me in full Granny disguise to her in prison. I'm sure she'd love to see how she inspired us! It's perfect timing that the news we apprehended her hasn't been announced. Nobody suspects a thing."

GUILTY ALERT! I was right! Elle had just admitted to pretending to be a fake Granny and – unbelievable! – they hadn't told anyone they'd caught the real Granny so they could blame the whole thing on her!

Poppy was silently mouthing 'No way' to me and Violet looked furious that we had been tricked by detectives we admired and had been trying to impress all week!

"Och, stop!" Tartania said, laughing. "See you out there, Golden Granny! When I get back on stage I'll tell everyone we were called to a false alarm. The Mystic Moustache is on the move. Over and out."

Still chuckling to herself, Tartania heaved her tartan Mystery Kit off the floor, wobbled under its weight and shuffled out of the room.

We waited until her now unsteady footsteps had disappeared before we spoke.

"I ... she ... I ... I can't believe she and Elle think this is funny!" Violet spluttered.

I knew how Violet felt. I'd been jealous that the Bafflement Boys seemed to know where the Golden Granny was. Now I felt sorry for them – by the sounds of it, they were about to make a very public and very mistaken deduction.

"They've completely messed up our chances in the competition," Poppy exploded. "If they get away with this there will be no saving the Young Super Sleuth's Society. Not only did they allow the Mystic Moustache to be stolen, they didn't identify that their top detectives were to blame!"

"WE HAVE TO STOP THEM!" I said, racing from the dressing room.

run!

11:35AM
ON STAGE WITH A CRIMINAL DETECTIVE AND SUPER SLEUTHER COMPETITORS.

We sprinted onto the stage, leaves flying from our half-finished tree costumes, just in time to see Linus grab the microphone from Tartania – his Mystery Eyebrow still clearly visible, even though his face had been painted to blend perfectly into the detective featured in his disguise.

"Please remain calm,"
Linus's voice boomed.
"The Bafflement Boys
have discovered … "

"STOP!" I yelled. They might be our arch-rivals but it was only fair to save Linus the embarrassment of getting things wrong.

The audience shifted their gaze from Linus to me, Poppy and Violet. We looked as if we'd been dragged through a hedge, twigs sticking out of our hair and hanging uselessly from our tops.

I could see Mum, Dad and Arthur, all in their Mystery Girl support T-shirts, staring at me as if I'd totally lost it.

When I'd pictured what it would be like to be in the Super Sleuther final challenge, it hadn't been anything like this.

The Suspicious Sistas, now three sofas with only arms and legs sticking out, put their hands on their hips. Give Us a Clue turned to stare (with great difficulty in their stiff robot costumes). Darlene Dangerfield rolled her eyes and carried on applying white make-up to complete her frozen statue look.

Tartania stood, looking mildly surprised to see us. She obviously thought she and Elle were going to get away with the whole thing.

Poppy tilted her head slightly in the direction of Tartania's Mystery Kit, letting me know it was tucked at the side of the Suspicious Sistas' dressing room. Good. Elle hadn't made her escape with the Moustache yet.

Even though this was
a tense situation, I had
the weird urge to laugh
when I saw that Pip had
been painted to look
like an old-fashioned
lady detective. Pip did
not look as if he thought
this was funny; he looked
furious. Linus shot us a
warning glance that said, don't
you dare ruin my Big Reveal!

"As I was saying," he continued. "The Bafflement
Boys are pleased to announce that we have
tracked down the Mystic Moustache, which was
stolen by master criminal, the Golden Granny!"

There was a shocked gasp from the audience and
the other competitors.

"The Golden Granny is using the oldest trick in the book, hiding right under our noses, here on stage!" Linus said, looking smugger than ever, even though he had no idea what was really going on.

I didn't even feel a bit smug myself that Linus was mostly wrong. I just wished the real Golden Granny had been behind this whole thing and that Elle Lusive and Tartania McSnuff could still be my heroes.

Pip pointed dramatically to a closed door in the wall at the side of the stage. We'd walked past that to get on stage and I'd assumed it must just contain props. I knew it definitely did not contain the Golden Granny.

mysterious door

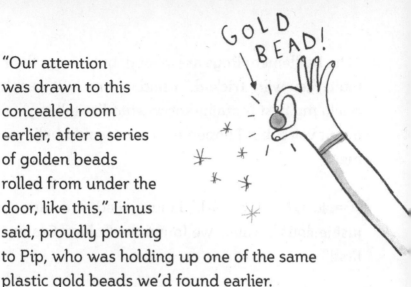

GOLD BEAD!

"Our attention was drawn to this concealed room earlier, after a series of golden beads rolled from under the door, like this," Linus said, proudly pointing to Pip, who was holding up one of the same plastic gold beads we'd found earlier.

Tartania took a few theatrical steps back from the door. Now that I knew the truth, I could see that she was faking it.

Poppy and Violet looked unsure what to do next but I realised why beads had been rolling out of that room. While Linus paused for dramatic effect, I raced forward and grabbed the microphone. (His detective reactions were very poor because it was easy.)

"The Bafflement Boys are wrong, but it's not their fault, they were tricked," I said in a rush. It wasn't really my best I-totally-know-what-I'm-talking-about voice, but I hoped everyone would believe me.

"Get lost, Mystery Girl!" Linus yelled. "You are just jealous because we found the Golden Granny first!"

Poppy and Violet tried their best to block his attempts to snatch the microphone back.

my best
take me
seriously
face

"The Golden Granny is not in that room. Elle Lusive, disguised as the Golden Granny is," I continued. "Elle Lusive and Tartania McSnuff stole the Mystic Moustache and made it look like the Golden Granny took it!"

There was no gasp. Just a shocked, uncomfortable silence.

I glanced at Tartania McSnuff, who, weirdly, was now grinning at me. She clearly thought that by acting innocent, nobody would believe me. I waved at the tartan Mystery Kit by the side of the Suspicious Sistas' dressing room. Violet was there in seconds.

Grinning

I pictured her lifting out the trophy and holding it up for everyone to see, but it was so heavy that all Violet managed to do was heave it out of the bag before she fell over backwards.

The golden gleam of the Mystic Moustache was unmistakable, though! There was a sharp intake of breath from everyone in the audience.

"WHAT'S GOING ON?!" Darlene Dangerfield yelled.

"Unless I'm very much mistaken, Elle Lusive was about to run out of that room dressed as the Golden Granny before disappearing," I said. "That way you'd all believe that the Golden Granny had escaped with the Mystic Moustache and nobody would suspect Elle and Tartania are actually the thieves! When they were long gone you'd all find out that it couldn't have been the Golden Granny, because she is already in prison!"

I tried to fix my best don't-mess-with-me Mystery Girl stare on Tartania, but it was hard to maintain because she had started doing some sort of weird Scottish dance.

"YIPPEEE!" she said, leaping from one foot to the other.

What sort of deranged criminal were we dealing with?

CRAZY

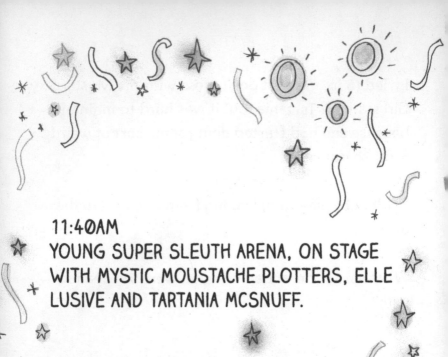

11:40AM
YOUNG SUPER SLEUTH ARENA, ON STAGE
WITH MYSTIC MOUSTACHE PLOTTERS, ELLE
LUSIVE AND TARTANIA MCSNUFF.

WAHH WAHH WAHH!

A deafening siren sounded.

BOOM!

A cloud of golden confetti fired from
above our heads. The stage plunged
into darkness and hundreds of disco
lights flashed a blinding purple and
pink. Was this some sort of cunning cover
so that Lusive and McSnuff could escape?

The sirens fell silent and the dancing disco lights froze. I tried to get my balance and, through the slowly falling cascade of distracting confetti, I saw the Golden Granny – or should I say, Elle Lusive – in full golden costume, cartwheeling towards Tartania from the now-open door of the room at the side of the stage.

Before I could attempt to chase her, she flipped upright. She and Tartania both looked totally excited, even though I'd just destroyed their detective reputations.

My Mystery Senses told me something weird was going on.

"Ah, Mystery Girls!" said Tartania, beaming. "We can reveal that you have not been investigating a real-life crime! You have actually been solving a mystery set up by myself and Elle which was, in fact ..."

Wig

"... The Expect the Unexpected Challenge!" Elle finished, throwing her golden wig in the air in celebration.

WHAT!? The Expect the Unexpected Challenge had been cancelled, hadn't it?

"This was our hardest Expect the Unexpected Challenge yet, because none of you knew it was happening," Tartania said. "We faked the theft of the Mystic Moustache and knew only the most daring detective agencies would attempt to open an investigation, taking their full concentration away from becoming Super Sleuther Champion."

Could Elle and Tartania be telling the truth?

"Well done, Bafflement Boys and Mystery Girls, for taking that risk. We set up a false trail leading, as you know, to the Golden Granny," Elle said.

"We expected some of you to guess that the Granny was the chief suspect, and maybe one or two of you to find where she was hidden," Tartania continued, beaming. "But even a fully qualified Super Sleuth would struggle to figure out that we were the ones behind the whole thing!"

"We would have told you the truth, of course, after the Bafflement Boys had exposed me," Elle said. "Congratulations to the Bafflement Boys for spotting those golden beads I was rolling under the door. And congratulations, Mystery Girls, for displaying some of the most advanced young detective work I have ever seen!"

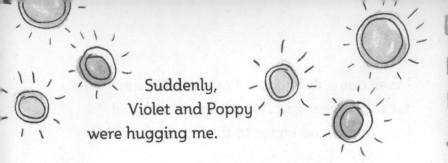

Suddenly,
Violet and Poppy
were hugging me.

"Did you hear what Elle said, Mariella?" Poppy said. "Being a proper Young Super Sleuther is all about thinking like a professional detective and that's what we did!"

The audience had started clapping and whooping now and I couldn't help smiling. This week had been the most stressful ever, but I was relieved that it was still OK to want to be just like Elle and Tartania when I'm older. And actually, from what Tartania said, we aren't that far off!

"So, hang on – there was never a Golden Granny?" Linus said. For the first time, his Mystery Eyebrow had fallen into the eyebrow position of a normal person.

"Linus!" Pip shouted. He looked horrified and was pointing madly at Linus's forehead. Linus quickly repositioned something so his eyebrow was back suspended near his hairline.

I could see now that all this time the perfect
Bafflement Boy Eyebrows were just normal
eyebrows that had been stuck in place – with
sticky tape. Ha!

normal
eyebrows

tape!

"Mystery Girls, you have been awarded
quadruple points for working out what Elle and
I were up to – and for having the courage to
confront us about it," Tartania said.

"And Bafflement Boys, you are the winners of the
Disguise Challenge!" Elle said. "Which means
that this year we have joint Young Super Sleuther
Champions!"

The audience whooped
and cheered again and more
golden confetti fell. Poppy and
Violet jumped up and down. I could
see Mum, Dad and Arthur sitting in the front
row, proudly showing off the T-shirts Arthur
had made to people sitting nearby.

As I was still holding a microphone, this
seemed like a good opportunity to give an
excellent Young Super Sleuth Champion sort
of closing speech.

But all that came out was,
"ARRGGGHHHHEEEE! THE MYSTERY GIRLS
ARE SUPER SLEUTH WINNERS! Oh, and so
are the Bafflement Boys. YEAHHHHH!"

Oh well, I'd been working
hard at being
professional all
week. Now it was
time to PARTY!

Friday
10TH August

We did it!

chilling

3:00PM
MYSTERY GIRL HQ, CHILLING ON A BEANBAG.

When I woke up this morning I thought I
must have dreamed all the amazing stuff that
happened yesterday. Then I realised my pillow
was covered in golden confetti that had been
stuck in my hair and that my face felt numb
because I'd rolled onto the rubber winner's
Mystic Moustache trophy. (I'd fallen asleep
holding it. Now I've got it,
I don't want to let it
go.) Conclusive proof
that the best day of
my detective career
so far totally did
happen!

Rubber
replica!

After the cheering stopped, all
the contestants were whisked to
the Young Super Sleuth Experience
Famously Infamous Hall for a party. The exhibits
had been pushed to the sides of the room, there
was a smoke machine set to maximum power
and a shimmering golden dance
floor. (Embarrassingly, Arthur
decided to start dancing
like a crazy person way
before anyone else did,
but I tried not to let that
distract me from the
amazingness of the
situation.)

embarrassing!

The Mystic Moustache
glittered as the disco lights reflected off it. I
couldn't believe the Mystery Girls were going
to have their names engraved on it – especially
since, just a few hours before, I'd been certain
we'd come last. It was such an unbelievable
feeling, I didn't even care that the Bafflement
Boys were joint winners.

The Suspicious Sistas came over and started high-fiving us, saying that if we wanted to we could definitely become Suspicious Sistas. I said thanks for the offer, but the Mystery Girls would be staying mysterious for now. (For ever, actually.)

Give Us a Clue didn't seem to care who'd won, not after they saw the massive buffet of mysterious golden food – golden moustache-shaped biscuits and egg mayonnaise sandwiches and sausage rolls!

golden biscuits   golden sandwiches   golden sausage rolls

You'd think the Bafflement Boys would have been a bit more cheerful, but they just sat in the corner looking fed up.

Violet said that professional detectives (which we have proved we are) maintain good relationships with fellow mystery-solvers, even suspicious-smarty-pants annoying ones, and I knew she was right, so we went to speak to them.

Linus and Pip said congratulations and forced a smile. Then they said they'd been wrong to say the Mystery Girls would never be as good as the Bafflement Boys, because we officially were as good as them.

I really wanted to say that OF COURSE we are as good as them – actually, loads better – but instead I said we'd let them know if there were any smaller cases we didn't have time to take on, because figuring out the whole Golden Granny mystery might make us world-famous detectives in massive demand. Ha!

World Famous
mystery Girls

The best bit of the whole party was when Elle and Tartania came over to congratulate us again.

Elle said the Mystery Girls had reminded her that a true Master of Disguise shouldn't cut any corners, and that she didn't know what she'd been thinking, wearing fake plastic golden beads and buying a cheap wig that shed hair. Then she winked and said that she knew who to call if she needed help with any investigations. WOW!

I've just finished writing up our case report. It's going to appear in the *Puddleford Gazette*! Soon everyone in Puddleford will know the full story of how the Mystery Girls figured out who stole – or didn't really steal – the Mystic Moustache.

CASE REPORT: THE MISSING MYSTIC MOUSTACHE

The Mystic Moustache's theft was, in fact, staged by Young Super Sleuth's Society representatives, Elle Lusive and Tartania McSnuff, as part of a top-secret Expect the Unexpected Challenge, designed to test Young Super Sleuther competitors to the absolute limits of their mystery-solving abilities.

Elle and Tartania called a break after the first challenge, not so they could decide who had won, but so that they could stage the theft of the Mystic Moustache!

Unlike previous years, the Expect the Unexpected Challenge was far more difficult because everyone was led to believe that it had been cancelled to allow Elle and Tartania to focus on finding out who took the Moustache.

Detective Sparks from Puddleford police is a huge fan of Elle and Tartania's work, so agreed to go along with the investigation to make the theft seem more convincing and to play a part in training the next generation of detectives.

toffee

wrapper

The trail of strange golden clues we were following - which we thought belonged to the individual who'd stolen the Mystic Moustache - were totally and utterly fake. The trail pointed to the Golden Granny - an infamous criminal with an obsession for stealing all things golden.

false teeth

gold fluff

tea

Elle Lusive disguised herself as the Golden Granny, appearing in various places around Puddleford. She lived up to her reputation as a master of disguise with a costume and acting ability that was almost flawless. But 'almost' isn't good enough when the Mystery Girls are around.

We were the only detective agency to notice that some of the Golden Granny's actions seemed a bit odd, even for her, and we spotted clues Elle and Tartania never meant us to find. In her rush to get changed, golden beads, hair and dust fell unnoticed from Elle's costume, just outside the judges' dressing room.

A search led to the discovery of the missing trophy and Elle's Golden Granny disguise. Closer examination revealed her golden jewellery was actually made from plastic. The Granny only wears real gold, so we knew it couldn't be hers.

Plastic

The only conclusion the Mystery Girls were able to draw was that Elle Lusive and Tartania McSnuff were mystery-solvers turned bad, and that it was them, not the Golden Granny, who had stolen the Mystic Moustache - and so we were faced with accusing our heroes of being criminals.

guilty

Even though our fellow young detectives (well, mostly the Bafflement Boys) thought we were totally crazy, we confronted Elle and Tartania and received quadruple points for not only following the false trail, but for being brave and professional enough to expose the truth - or what we thought was the truth.

innocent!
PHEW!

(It was an excellent way to practise our skills, revealing a dramatic scandal without actually having to see the reputations of our hero detectives ruined. YAY!)

CASE CLOSED.

NOTE: We've suggested to Elle and Tartania that they need to read contestant application forms more thoroughly in future. They obviously hadn't read the Mystery Girls' application form well enough - then they would have known that nothing gets past us! Plastic gold beads! What was Elle thinking?

This is the photo taken just after we won - it's our best Just Solved the Case photo yet! I might even get it printed on a T-shirt!

mystery Girl winners!

ACKNOWLEDGEMENTS

I'd like to say a huge thank you to the people who have helped me live in a world of intrigue and fake moustaches while creating Mariella Mystery's world.

A massive Mystery Girl high five for my editor Jenny Glencross, who I have learned so much from and who always has a stunner of an idea in her Mystery Kit. I'm grateful for her time, patience and commitment to Super Sleuthing.

A top secret handshake for the team at Orion for their support, enthusiasm and hard work in making Mariella an international mystery solver. Mystic Moustache awards also go to my agent, Mark, for starting me on this amazing journey and to my husband Simon, for helping to clear my brain of red herrings and being very understanding that a detective's work is never done.

This message will self destruct in five ... four ... three ... two ...